The Book of
Lamach of Cain
A Pseudepigrapha

By Pauly Hart

Published by Pauly Hart Art
Printed in the USA, where available.
ISBN: 978-1-955399-50-0

Cover art and design by Pauly Hart
Editing by Jennifer Hart

For information about the author, please visit PaulyHart.com
Library of Congress Catalog Data is available at: Loc.gov
This book is available on Amazon.com and wherever fine books are sold.

For those who seek

"And Cain knew his wife; and she conceived, and bare Enoch: and he builded a city, and called the name of the city, after the name of his son, Enoch. And unto Enoch was born Irad: and Irad begat Mehujael: and Mehujael begat Methusael: and Methusael begat Lamech.

And Lamech took unto him two wives: the name of the one *was* Adah, and the name of the other Zillah. And Adah bare Jabal: he was the father of such as dwell in tents, and *of such as have* cattle. And his brother's name *was* Jubal: he was the father of all such as handle the harp and organ. And Zillah, she also bare Tubal-Cain, an instructer of every artificer in brass and iron: and the sister of Tubal-Cain *was* Naamah.

And Lamech said unto his wives, Adah and Zillah, Hear my voice; ye wives of Lamech, hearken unto my speech: for I have slain a man to my wounding, and a young man to my hurt. If Cain shall be avenged sevenfold, truly Lamech seventy and sevenfold."

Genesis 4:17-24 KJV

INTRODUCTION AND PREFACE

Dearest Reader,

History tells us little of the trials and tribulations of people in the sidelines of the Bible. Often, we are left to our own devices to try to discover or just imagine what happened to them. We are left with love stories and hero's journeys of many outliers. So and so's cousin who once met king David or so and so who was second cousin to Hezekiah and how they fell in love with so and so. It's great fun as a writer to do all the research and determine how to weave your stuff into the actual stuff seamlessly. Great fun and, of course, everyone knows it's fiction and so we leave it at that. It gets a great cover and it's sold in Christian stores everywhere.

I remember being at Mardel's in Tulsa, Oklahoma, walking down the aisle looking at all the market shares going towards… Well, mostly middle aged white stay-at-home mothers. Great market and nothing wrong with that. All they had for me was Frank Peretti and a little Stephen R. Lawhead, until Christian distributors decided to ban him and pick up Ted Dekker, who was mostly unknown at the time. And that was it for me. Nothing on par with Robert Heinlein or Ben Bova, or, God forbid, George RR Martin. Oh sure, Tolkien and Lewis were OK, but not the other Inklings like Charles Williams. Tulsa couldn't handle anything more metaphysical than a Charismatic prayer line. 'Sorry Pauly Hart,' Mardels said, 'Nothing outside Sunday School for you.'

What a pity. From 1990-1995 I attended Bible College in Tulsa and there wasn't a lot to sink my teeth into, fantastically literature-wise. So I read the Bible a lot. I also read Larry Niven, Joe Haldeman, Freed, Azimov, Brin, and my two favorites Harry Harrison and

Robert Asprin. The internet wasn't really a place to find books back then and great Christian fiction sort of circulated from friend to friend instead of kindle to kindle. But I really wanted to read more Lawhead, so I went to Barnes and Nobles and picked up Lawhead's Pendragon Cycle, which blew my mind. Taliesin and Merlin were literally life changing.

Why dismiss anything not taught by Wesely or Luther? Why hold suspect all the impossible things we already take for granted inside of belief in the Bible? What is harder to believe? That giants walked the earth, or that the literal voice of The Intelligent Designer became sentient, came to earth, was born of a virgin, and died on a Roman torture device, only to be resurrected so that The Intelligent Designer could remarry his divorced wife, Israel? I'd say it's easier to believe in abnormally tall men instead of the other one. But, the belief in the other one is a requirement to become metaphysically reborn and have your spirit enter into the third heaven… So, no giants then. Seems ludicrous that the leaders of "Christianity" over the years have divorced us so far away from the other supernatural elements of the faith.

One of the largest lies perpetrated on the Christian people, or, the modern Ekklesia, is that the true Genesis 6 viewpoint takes all of the supernatural elements away from the invention of Demonology. Augustine preached the Sethian view of Genesis 6 came about when the Sons of Adam took the Daughters of Cain and made children, literally handicapping the most supernatural elements of the faith… Taking the lies of man and reading them back into the text. I choose to allow the Bible to interpret the Bible, as good exegesis allows. When taken on a face-value basis, we see that the first incursion of the Sons of God (The Bene' Elohim) having relations with The Daughters of Men (Mankind) and by them created monsters. As the Bible says, "giants of whom stories are told." Dr. Michael Heiser, in his book <u>Reversing Hermon</u> does a great job destroying the Sethite viewpoint. Worth a read, if you're interested in some very valuable viewpoints on exegetical interpretation of the spiritual views of the ancient Hebrew writer.

This book differs greatly from many viewpoints handed down from Augustine, who paved the way for the Sethite view. The way I treat my theology these days is pretty simple. I imagine that I've never read any of the several thousand works by other authors explaining what the Bible says to me. I pretend that I've never gone to school for apologetics, hermeneutics, homiletics, eschatology, christology, missiology, or church polity. I pretend that I've found myself on a desert island with the Protestant Canon of 70 books (Psalms being 5 books), a notebook, and a thousand pencils. I'd read the thing again and again and started writing my questions down.

One of the most interesting things I've come to believe in this process, is how much I've been lied to. At the same time that I've been writing this, I've also been writing a conversational story called <u>An Uncomfortable and Disastrous Creature</u>, where I discuss many of the theological ideas that appear here, including several that do not. I'll guarantee some of the things in this book you'll not have heard before.

The first of which (in agreement) is that there are more than just "Angels" who are supernatural beings. We've read about Cherubim and Seraphim and have maybe thought about the fiery chariots who took Elijah up to heaven. Were they drawn by heavenly horses? And we've heard of others in the Bible, but we haven't talked about them. There are Watchers and Princes, who are not men, but spiritual entities. There are also the sons of the Watchers, the Nephilim (Anakim, Goliath, Og of Bashan, etc...) who are the bodied and disembodied spirits of the union from the Sons of God and the Daughters of Men. If the Bible talks about all of these beings, then they just might be important.

Leviticus 16:8 reads: "And Aaron shall cast lots for the two goats, one lot for Yahweh and the other lot for Azazel." Who in the world is Azazel? Could he be one of the Watchers mentioned in Daniel 4:17? "This decision is the decree of the Watchers, the verdict declared by the holy ones, so that the living will know that the Most High rules over the kingdom of mankind and gives it to whom He wishes, setting over it the lowliest of men."

The Book of Enoch, is not found in the Protestant Canon, however it is found in the Ethiopian Coptic Canon. Azazel is mentioned heavily in Enoch and his saga takes place in Enoch chapters 8-13. I'm not here to defend a pro-Enoch canon stance, but we do find evidence of these celestial, astral, angelic, and sometimes demonic entities all over ancient writings. If the Bible says they exist, then why are we so quick to dismiss other witnesses as heretical?

This is why the misunderstanding about the king of Tyre and the Prince of Tyre in Ezekiel 28 occurs. In the first two parts out of the total four parts of the chapter we have two laments. The first lament is for the human ruler of Tyre and the second lament is for the spiritual ruler of Tyre. They cannot be the same person for the first person is said to have wanted to be a spiritual elohim while being a mere man. The second person is said to actually be a cherub. Obviously this is referring to two people. The lament is for the totality of the ruling reign of Tyre. The human and the spiritual will both diminish. The King of Tyre fell, as well as the Prince of Tyre. The Prince fell just as many of the Watchers fell.

Historians aren't often Spirit-inspired but in a few instances, they are. The writer Luke, who wrote the gospel by his name and also the book of Acts of the Apostles, was. Most of us would agree that Josephus was not, even though quite literally, Josephus wrote ten times the amount that Luke did. One would argue that this book, though obviously a pseudepigrapha, is quite impactful, though it's size is similar to Luke or Acts. A Christmas Carol by Charles Dickens was under 29 thousand words and Animal Farm by George Orwell was under 30 thousand. Often, the story is long enough without the texture of added fluff.

My wife is an avid reader but cannot stand my writing. She tells me to write more about the color of the leaves in spring, as the dew gently clings to the fragrant rose petals; all I'm interested in is the monster ehind it who's about to eat the protagonist. *C'est la vive.* I've become a better writer because of her, and cannot thank her enough for her help in proofing and editing many of my works in the past. Her tireless and indefatigable patience is a blessing that I do not know how to go without.

In my last pseudepigrapha, which you should go out right now and buy, by the way, Enoch is commanded by Yahweh to go and measure Salem. When he arrives, Melchesideck ministers to him and they talk for a while. After this, Enoch is led by a Seraph and visits the Egyptian city of Thinis, who was built by the giants of old, sons of the Watchers. Kidnapped by Osiris, he must deal with the Watchers and proclaim the Day of The Lord. It's a fun romp and it's one of the most exciting projects I've ever worked on.

This book is kinda like that. Hope you love it.

-Pauly Hart

ADAM VISITS LAMACH

Hither came Adam, the king of the garden of The Creator, black of hair, staff in hand on yonder road. And he saw me sitting on my stool carving a rune upon the rocks.

Now I, Lamach, was dwelling outside the city gate of Enoch to the south, at the gate Samlazaz.

"Lo, seed of Cain." He said to me.

"What ho, king Adam." I replied. "If you seek your son, he is not here, he is camped on the north side of the city."

"And what is your name?" The king asked.

"I am Lamach, of Mehu-Sael, of Mehu-Jael, of Irad, of Enoch, of Cain."

"Of me, of Hashem Adonai El-Elyon, Maker of all." The king said, looking at the city and the gates, thoughtfully. "There are many men of Cain here?" He asked. "In truth, I have not been here before."

"Yes. Of Enoch, and his other sons, Olad, Lizaph, Fosal, and of his daughters, Citha and Maac. All of Cain, all of you."

Saying to me now: "See now how your land prospers while my rib lays forlorn in a cave. See now the beautiful walls your city has while I have but a lonely cave. Though Hashem Adonai El-Elyon has made it for us, we do not feel Him there nor hear Him any more. I am lost, I am alone in my troubles and I do not wish to speak my rib, for she only dwells on the things that she does not have and not on the things that she does."

He sat at my feet and began to cry. I knew not of his troubles, for I had troubles of my own, and he lived some distance to the west. I had been alone the whole of the day until the king of Eden came to me. The manner that was his was not something that we sons of Cain shared. I had never seen a man weeping this way and it sat in my gullet as a sour stone.

"What leads you here to me? To this place?" I questioned him, for I was indeed curious as to his visit.

"You are the seventh from Cain so therefore you are almost as if you had not a curse nor a mark upon you. If you are Lamach then the seventh from The Creator after me. You have children, do you not?" king Adam asked me.

"Indeed I have five children from my two wives. Three sons and two daughters."

"Five!" The king exclaimed. "And I had but two hands to wrestle my two seeds!" He exclaimed again, "And I was wondering at how I could bear it." So I told him.

"Two wives is my secret. One for the fire, and one for the field. With one wife there is trouble, but with two wives there is so very much more. In truth, to keep them apart with much busy work means that I have peace to carve upon the rock or tree."

"In truth, there is always trouble for me. For to live with a woman such as mine bears the bones into water. My rib does frown and weep. She does not know happiness since the day Hashem Adonai El-Elyon took vengeance upon us for our sin in Eden."

"Is it the happiness of a former life or of a former husband?" I asked, to which he had no response and for long hours he laid his head on my feet saying this and that on his life's hardships.

ADAM WEEPS

Thereupon lay the king of earth and of the garden on my feet weeping for a day.

"Teach me how to live again, Lamach, for you are alive and hale and have a whole life around you."

"You do not know what goes on in the city. For though I have pitched my tent towards Enoch, I desire not the small things within its gates. Their ways are small and not mine but I have no other people. I spend my time with the expanse. As you are here, the Morning Stars come and talk. But when I do not talk with the greater ones, I am alone with bow and with arrow… With tree and bird. These fields are my friends."

"You remind me so very much of Cain in that way. Though he was never a-seated as you, but always running here or there with every odd herb, finding its ways and if it be chaff or if it was to eat." The king said.

"I carve upon the rocks and I work the tree, for this is my calling. Your seed works the earth. But you worked with the earth as well?" I asked.

"Nay, for my love was that of all the animals of the land. For they came to me and I named them." The king replied. "My rib and seed worked the land with joy. For me it is toil, still."

"For me, to work the land is toil, still. See the wonders I make in but a few simple hands of Shemesh? I cannot wait to see what my hands do next upon the rock or the tree, for when I carve, it is as the carving is growing on its own, and my hands are just there to bring it into the world."

"My rib thought the same of the bean and the leaf." Adam said. "Even before I renamed her to Eve, she was entranced with all things that were plucked from the ground."

"Your rib had another name?" I asked

"Ishah, my beloved self, the other me. The rib taken from me to be placed in the garden of His delight. When we left, I called her Hawwah, the living one, for she lived though she deluded The Creator in her dealings with The Dragon."

"I did not know you had named her after you had named all other animals." I said.

"Verily. For I loved her enough to name her twice." He said, sadly.

LAMACH COMFORTS THE KING

The whole of the town came to see the wonder of the king who visited me. Some brought gifts and others brought food.

My wives and many others had come to console him but he bid them away.

First my wife Ada came to him, she who had bore me Jubal and Jabal. She had brought fresh maize cakes and barley bread, for there were many bakers in the city, but Cain farmed all the fields.

The king would have naught to do with her, sending her away, saying, "For no, you shall not comfort me but only that which Hashem Adonai El-Elyon has given me shall be my burden."

"But these are cakes and breads that thy own son has grown. Eat, Lord king Adam, for the days must be long for you and the nights even longer, now that you have forsaken your beloved." Ada pleaded, coming close to him with her groin.

"Nay! Let it not be so!" Said the king. "For eternity she was created only to have me, and I in return will only have her. This is my will."

But I persisted in it. "Let it be so, Lord king, for my wife does many pleasures." And she opened her womb to him as I bade her do.

As did my wife Zillah and I, myself, offered myself to him to bring him comfort.

And he pushed us all away and would have no more comfort from us.

"You are as sinful as your father and your father's father!" He cried aloud to us. Grabbing up his staff he went to the sheep pen in back of my tent and slept there, as it was nightfall.

THE KING PLEADS

Early in the morning the king cried from outside my tent: "Lamach! Give me bread and water and take me to my son, for I wish to speak with him this day!"

So my wives brought out the bread from yesterday and cool water from a jug and he ate and drank and said his thanks and would be on his way that very moment but did not know where he would go except around the city to the other side and I bade him tarry for a moment while I gathered my family and so I took the king and my family to go see my forefather and his father and what might be said between them.

And Cain was working the field with his many plants.

And when the king was a far way off the king saw Cain and cried aloud with his voice -

"Son of my rib, will you see your father?"

And Cain did not respond so the king approached closer and cried again -

"Seed of my loins, will you see your father?"

And Cain still did not respond but picked up his staff and smote the ground.

Thus king Adam held fast his ground and cried aloud yet again, "It is with distress that I come to you! For your mother has laid herself up in a cave. I fear she will not move again to work or to even see the rising or setting of the sun, such is her distress all these years."

Cain said nothing.

"And she cries for the great sin she committed upon me with the chief of the ha-Satan, Leviathan. And she cries for the great sin she committed towards Hashem Adonai El-Elyon. And she cries for thee and for thy brother and for the lost world we left before you were born. Will you see her or send word of your well-doing so that I might return to her and tell her that, at least, here in this place, you have found some solace in the earth that The Creator has made? Will you come with me as I go to her in consolation?"

Cain said nothing still.

"And if you will not come with me, then will you bring all you have and move towards us at least a little so that if she desires so, she might see the works of your hands and the children of her childs loins? Cain! My son! My only child of my flesh! Will you come see the woman who gave you life? For I may wander the lands here and there and see the men of the earth, but your mother and I are children of the garden and not children of earth. For we desire to sup with you as we did in your young years, and for you to tell us of the grasses and plants and all the things you found in the forest while you played there with the wolf and the lambs. I have forgiven the sins of the past and ask that you accept us once again into your heart."

CAIN RESPONDS

But Cain stood his ground, and taking his crook, he broke it in two, and declared:

"This is the land I was driven to in my chastisement for my sin. See what I have made of the place! And with my son Enoch and his sons and their sons we are now a city against The Creator, for this city is named after my son Enoch. It is my city, it is his city and The Creator is not here. The Creator is not allowed here, for we create what we want. We are just in that. But The Creator is a treacherous creator, unjust in all His ways."

The king answered Cain, "In goodness the world was created. And it's managed by the fruit of good works. There's no level of respect in judgment. The fruits of good work are better than evil. A gift of love is accepted over one of hate with good will."

But Cain said: "There isn't judgment or Judge, or another world. No reward is given to the righteous. No revenge is taken by the wicked. The world wasn't created in goodness, and it's not run in goodness. It was my brother's gift that was accepted with good will, and mine that wasn't accepted with good will."

Then the king said to Cain, "There is a judgment and there is a Judge. And there is another world. There is a good judgment given to the righteous, and a vengeful judgment taken on the wicked. In goodness, the world was created, and in goodness, it's conducted.

It's ruled by the fruit of good works. Because Able's were better than yours, his offering was accepted. The judge is love and everyone who lives in love, lives in The Judge and The Judge lives in them. As we then live in The Judge, our love grows more perfect even as we see the day of judgment approaching. So then we do not have to be afraid of the day of judgment but we can face The Judge with confidence because we live through His Word in this world."

But Cain spat on the ground and pointed behind the king.

"See then how my offering is accepted now, first man of the garden! For I have taken a wife with the first men of the earth and begotten a family. Herein is my inheritance, and herein is my grace, that the goodness I make is the goodness that I take for myself. I bear the very mark on my head and hands that no one should kill me but my family bears no such mark. So I am judge and high ruler over the world I have carved."

THE CITY BEARS WITNESS

At this time, the whole city had come to Cain's field to view the spectacle that was the king standing and talking to their forefather and father. Enoch was there, ere the priest in white, while his seed, Irad, who stood in workers clothes, ere the builder with his work apron and chisel and measuring rod. All men had stopped their workings to come see the king and his seed. Mehu-Jael and Mehu-Sael stood by, consorts from the men of the earth in hand, on their arms, naked with painted bodies.

Sariel stood behind Mehu-Jael and Mehu-Sael, stroking both men's hair, muttering. His blue form glowing. And there was a silver thread in my vision that led to the heavens and yet no man saw it and it was from Sariel from the very top of his head and led to the second heaven where Raphael stood watching. And I told no man this.

But as I looked to the vault I beheld Semjaza and Azazel standing in a cloud consorting with one another. They spoke to each other as men who give dark sayings, heads close, eyes on the earth and upon Cain and upon the king.

And their sons and daughters stood round, not interfering in what were the goings on, for they knew they were not invited. Their array of faces, heads, and bodies, some part dragon, some part beast, some part beast with heads of men, and others whose parts were parts of things not imagined. And also the beasts who were giants were there, fully hadam in feature but overly large and foreboding.

My family and all others families were there, but of Tubal-Cain, my son, I saw not.

Then the people clamored for the king to become their king that they might have the first man from the garden as their ruler, but of the ruling, the Adam did not seem like they would take part in his guidance, but he allowed it saying: "But who knows that I have come to this place for such a time as this?" Though no one but me heard him utter the words.

A HOUSE FOR THE KING

There had been erected a centerpiece into the altar and Semjaza called on the people there to fit the king a house in the city. And he called all animals and all the Watchers and of all the earth, the beasts of the field and of the waters, and the untold beasts from the Watchers brood. And of the birds and great serpents of the air, sea and all that is on them and in them. And many came, for Semjaza had called to the wastes of Dudael and past Eden and to all the four extremities of the earth, and had asked if the king could not rule among his people.

And so Azazel the goat demon Watcher and Semjaza, the shining one of perdition, sought among the whole of the earth permission for Adam to reign and rule over them all.

And it seemed good to all the hadam of the earth for them to have the Adam of the garden rule over them. And it seemed good to all the seed of Cain that the king would rule over them instead of Cain. Yet the seed of the king refused to come into the gates of the city and plowed the field alone and his wife and all others who visited him. Many other children he bare but would dash upon the rocks if they were the seed of the Watchers, for his desire was to have no more of their kind, though they bore more and more children to the women with each passing of Shemesh and Nanna. For violence, Cain showed love, but for the children of men, he showed none.

Semjaza spoke: "It is to Him who we appeal and when the time is upon us to do this or to do that. Whatever we behold we shall do, and whatever vows we take to each other we shall do them in front of the Adam, who is our rightful king of Enoch, for in this city you have built a place for him already, though you did not know it."

And the words of Semjaza seemed good to the seed of Cain and they built him a house and a throne on top of the house so that he should rule. And the house was built on top of a cave near the middle of the city, so that the heat of the day and cool of the night interfered not. And it was Tubal-Cain, my seed, who was assisting Irad in the build.

And the house was started and finished in one day. But for the king's rib they did not build a bed.

And the king lay down to rest and in the habitat that had been built for him.

And Cain stood outside the gates.

And I slept outside the hou
se of the king Adam.

THE KING MEETS TUBAL-CAIN

When he awoke the king went to where there was a shrine to The Watcher Azazel, who had come to dwell in the city. Time and again he would leave and reckon upon the sons and daughters of Cain and see how they fared.

And his shrine was encased in a rock that glowed with the rising of the sun, for it was metalwork.

The king asked about such a thing and they told him that Tubal-Cain had made it and that he worked with metalwork.

So the king went to where Tubal-Cain was and inquired about him.

It was a far out place and there were many men and women arriving and starting laborious tasks.

And a great many Watchers were there also.

But they did not talk to the king and let him wander and appraise.

And as he was searching for Tubal-Cain, out of the ground came the man, for there were massive tunnels built there, where they might find the metals one could use to forge their metalwork. And there were rough forges and a great many trees had been felled to fuel the fires of the forges. And one of the Watchers showed them a way to ignite the fires into a glow so bright and a heat so hot that it rivaled Shemesh himself.

But if Shemesh was jealous of this, I had no way of knowing. For he and his band of sisters raced over us, day upon day, immune to our pleas and curses. Though the earth remained at rest, the hosts of heaven were never dullards. But here, among the diggers, the earth groaned.

My son Tubal-Cain was rough and very much like the king's son, in almost every way, except that he hid his sins behind his eyes, for indeed he was a devious and hateful man but his countenance was betrayal. His feet were swift to shed blood and his nose directed towards the haughty.

Such was my disappointment and disgust when it was, that Tubal-Cain threw his arms open wide to greet the king with the warm embrace of a lover. In betrayal of intent, he kissed him upon the face and declared that it would be a day of rejoicing and merriment that the great man of the garden, king of earth, had come to visit him in his humble venture.

"I do not come to visit you in happiness, son's son." king Adam said, "But in greeting me thus, you have quickened my heart in its sadness and have also given me an unknown relief, for you are very much like my firstborn, though his love was for the earth and not the things under the earth. Seeing you makes me weep for my loss, all the more. Seeing you is like seeing him, yet not seeing him at the same instance."

"But rejoice with us at any rate, oh king. For tonight we have our celebrations with The Watchers in our covenant of the accusers, for Semjaza will be sharing some drink with us cut from special roots and we will remember our covenant as it was, as if in a vision." Tubal-Cain said to the king, smiling.

But the king said: "I dare not take part in thy ritual." But Tubal-Cain heeded not.

THE MEN OF THE EARTH

And at this time, one of the wandering bands of the children of the Watchers came towards the city from the north. They had large clothes made of fur and they carried long beams tipped with pointed metalwork. They wore skulls from the animals and hadam that they killed, for to kill a hadam was not the sin of Cain, but was a sport to some and a meal to others. And they came, one score of them, with also men from Cain among them. They had upon their skin great scars and cuts and paint and had intermingled some of the cuts with the juice of plants and dyes so the marks were indelible upon their skin. And they were hideous to behold, for they were of the tribe of Fosal, Cain's fourth son, and they devoted all things that had the nephesh to destruction.

And they blinked not at the new stone house, nor at the king, but delivered their prey to the middle of the city. And their prey was a tribe. They brought in the wild pale men who were of the hadam of the earth to cavort with them and to do the things that the men and women of the city did with them. And they were a tribe, large of frame, with strange dull blue eyes of the sky, and they were afraid of the giants who herded them into the Leviathan gate, from the east. They were naked and one was covered in the great striped fur of the swamp panther and who had on him a stone knife with a wooden haft. Fosal led them and threw down the leader in front of one of the giants who stepped on his head like a gourd.

And Fosal tore from him the fur and threw it upon his altar, then the body of the leader. One of the women, with a large brow and tangled hair wailed and Baraquiel dispatched her and piled her upon the heap. Then a fire was raised by embers and the bodies were burned. The giants, the largest two of Semjaza's seed, divided up the men and women between the crowd who took them away to their houses.

And the king Adam was wroth with Fosal who forbade him from harming the men of the earth in the manner that was before him, but Fosal heeded him not. And at this, Enoch began a ceremony and a prayer to the great serpent, but the king conceded not to the ceremony and began to tear down the fire but ceased when he heard the moaning and cries from the houses around.

So was brought to Enoch a babe from the men of the earth and there, in the middle of the fire, Enoch raised a knife to plunge it into the heart of the child. But the king felt great sorrow and pity and cried aloud for them to stop their wickedness. And Enoch took the jeweled knife and thrust it down upon the child and the king fell down upon the face of the earth, stricken and wroth with the deeds of the Watchers and of the seed of Cain who fell in line with their foul acts.

TUBAL-CAIN BINDS THE KING

Then came those who were in league with the deeds of the Watchers, having approved of the ceremony and set themselves upon the king and bound him with manacles and chains of bright metalwork, the color of Shemesh, to which the king could not break free of them. And Tubal sat the king upon the throne on the top of his house so that he might see but not interfere.

And my son Tubal was seven times more evil than the men who were in the city. For he had seen all the evil that was in the earth and had made weapons and devices from the minds of the Watchers and fashioned them in metalwork. And they proceeded with the ceremony until the end of it, Tubal-Cain watching in approval.

Therefore after all this the king raised his voice aloud and proclaimed: "Woe to you, who go the way of Cain! For I declare to you this day! Do not be like Cain who followed evil and slew his brother! And why then did he slay him? For his deeds were evil, while those of his brother? Righteous. And why was his brother righteous? Because by faith Abel offered unto The Creator a more excellent sacrifice than Cain, by which he obtained witness that he was righteous when The Creator approved his offering! And by faith Abel still speaks even though he is dead." The king cried out and then looking westward, continued. "Oh great king of all the earth, I worship you in your marvelous light and your glory fills the earth! As the firmament declares your glory and the stars your metalwork, so then my heart rejoices in your voice! Find me here in this place of woe and perdition. For I am in your hands and you alone can be my help and shield."

But as he was saying these things, then came Irad and Fosal and picked him up and carried him into the lower part of his house and shut him in.

And they took the stone and laid it back over the entrance to the cave wherein they trapped him.

And all the city people cried aloud for him to be entombed there forever. "We have captured the king of the garden. Now we will have both a king and peace." They lifted their lament and prayer and praise unto the heavens. Not to the God who ruled them, but to the sky alone.

Then came Fosal with great shackles made of the bright metalwork, from the forge of Tubal, and clasp them together on the outside of the great stone they had laid there on the outside of his house as well. For the chamber of the deep part of his house, and the house and the throne above it were all of hewn stone, so that it was immovable by hand. But the sons of the Watchers could move it with the ease of a man moving a small stone, as it was that they had built this house and others like it just so. As they had built the other edifices around the city and the city walls and the gates and everything else that was stone, the giants had built them.

So during the time of his imprisonment, the king cried aloud to The Creator in a loud voice so that even his captors heard him and said many things to Him in prayer. But the giants outside the house of the king gathered up tallow and stopped up their ears.

CAIN RESCUES THE KING

The gate to the east was named The Leviathan Gate, for it was faced away from Eden towards the rising of Shemesh, and to the great water that led out to the deeps. To the south was the gate of Samlazaz, who we also called Enki, and his gate was in the south, for his power was from the ends of the earth. To the North was the Irad gate, for it was the name of Enoch's son, who later was called the Eridu gate. To the west was no gate, for that was the destination of Eden. It was blockaded and fortified and was ever in darkness for a great parapet that shaded the whole wall, even during the brightest noon. At the setting of Shemesh, the wall was in shade, ever blinding the last rays from showering the light of Eden.

And so it was that for three days and three nights the king stayed in the womb of the earth until Cain strode from the outer gates and came and said unto us: "Why has my father, the king, befallen this? Is it not known to you that he was the man of the garden? Do you not know that The Creator will smite us all surely for what you have done to him?"

And so it was thus that Cain was the savior of the king, for though he, along with us, had taken the oath against The Creator of the garden, he was not without the fear of The Creator of the garden still. And still he reviled us when no one moved to unlatch the chain or move the stone.

"Though I bear the mark of Tav upon my head, know ye not that it will be counted upon your head should you slay the king of the garden. For he is the first one taken off the earth to be placed there, as you know, you are in his bloodline, for the shame upon his head shall be the shame upon your head. For I told the maker that my sin was greater than I could bear because anyone who would find me would kill me. And he had grace upon me to give me the Tav between my eyelets and upon my right hand, here and here."

And Cain did show the mark on his forearm that he had covered since the day we had known him. And he took off the turban upon his head that he wore always. His long black hair cascaded down over his face. Uncovering his face he threw back his hair and there upon his brow was the mark of Tav and upon his right wrist was the mark of Tav. That any who saw the mark and who killed Cain would have vengeance upon them up to the seventh generation. For the vengeance of the All-Maker is ever sure but his grace is limited to seven generations.

For though the whole of the city had known of the curse, no man had spoken of it in open, and all knew not whether it be myth or lie, but as Cain showed us his markings, we fell mute before him.

LAMACH COMMITS THE SIN OF CAIN

There was no man then to speak to Cain, for we all knew of his markings but did not know what the markings meant, for Cain did not come into the city except to get provisions or to unload heavy baskets of his crops. He talked to no one except the rare instance where he would enter the city to take from among the captured women. One such woman was the daughter of Arakiel, whom was found often with Tubal-Cain, in the earth. The daughter was of large stature but not as the others that Semjaza's women bore, but she was fierce and took many to her bed. She bore the son of Cain and called him Fosal. And so it was that Cain sometimes spoke to Fosal, for he was a hunter and did not come into the city, but visited here and there and brought strange meat and people from the world to the city.

And Fosal stood before Cain and would not let him enter near to undo the great chains upon the door so Cain grappled with him demanding he let him release his father but Fosal drew his blade upon him and sought to kill him, because a great lust came upon him that he would commit upon his father the sin that he committed upon his brother. But Cain saw in the spirit that his bastard son had in him the way of the ha-Satan and struck him in the throat before Fosal's blade found his mark. And a great geyser of massy blood erupted from Fosal's mouth as his head rocked towards the sky, and he did fall forward, and his head landed first and became at rest at an unnatural angle.

Now this sparked a flood of shock through the crowd, for many people of the city were in attendance, as was all of Fosal's hunters, and they became outraged at the sight of Cain slaying his own son, and many drew their weapons and all became hostile to all. In the commotion, no one had understood that Cain did not the sin of Cain upon his own son, as he was bastard and not child of the garden, but Lizpa, son of Cain had laid with Citha, daughter of Cain and produced an abundance of children who were always in trouble somewhere, and, one of their brood was behind me during this time. And he was pushed into me and I did think something horrible was behind. Whirling with my knife at my waist, I caught him in his chest and he fell into my arms.

Now there was much clamor and here and there, there were people, and so no one had seen my deed except myself and the dying boy of whom I knew not his name, but only that his family had come from marriage once, from their mothers, of the women of the earth, and that, though they had different mothers, they were both the line of Cain not having once interbred with the Watchers or the children of the Watchers and so I had committed the sin of Cain, and to my knowledge I was the only one to have ever done it.

LAMACH MARKS HIS FAMILY

When I knew this, I dropped the boy to the ground, whose face was full of dread, drawing his cloak over his face. I ducked away, pulling the blade from his body. His muffled voice that of a sheep to slaughter.

With the town running to and fro, Cain stood by the house of the king defying all to stop him. With Fosal dead at his feet, no one else dared come near. And I fled the scene with no eyes upon me or the crumpled mass at my feet who was becoming quieter even as the moments passed. I ran back to my tent ere anyone would see me with the boy.

I drew my wives aside and said that they should gather our children together as the whole of the people drew the king out of the cave. I brought my family into the tent that Jabal had made for us. For he was the maker and master of cloth and rope and my tent and my wive's tents were the most luxurious tents in the whole city. So it was that others had made mud houses they fashioned themselves with walls that jutted this way and that, or they had the hewn stone houses the giants had built them. I had elected to stay on the flat ground a goodly distance away from all that the city had in itself, thus was the way of my doing. And I called my sons and my wives and said to them there:

"Sons of Lamech! Wives of Lamech! Hear my voice! Listen to my words! I haven't killed a man. I won't be punished for it as the sin of Cain is upon his head alone. I've never destroyed any man, young or old wherefore my children won't die from this dire punishment. Cain's sin was changed by his repentance for seven generations to me, Lamech. The punishment of the son who hasn't sinned. Let it be heard that this rule should be to 77 generations. The generations of Lamach are brought high upon the judgment for no man can do to them what they would do to others."

So then I shor the heads of myself and my wives using a new blade Tubal-Cain had wrought with his metalwork knife. Then I carved into the heads of my sons and of my wives the same mark that Cain had upon his head and upon our wrists that he had shown us. Using the blood of a pure black goat we sacrificed it to Enki on our altar to him. Taking the blood we smeared into our cuts so that they would remain marks forever. So then it was that my sons shor their own heads as well to show they stood with their father in the taking of the mark.

And it was Sabbath so Tubal-Cain's sister was not with us but was at the altar, in service to Semjaza, doing unto them the rites of Enki. So then did she remain without the mark and also with her hair.

THE KING REBUKES THE WATCHERS

And this was during the time of the king's travail for he had not known his wife for a space of many years. For in wandering the earth he had begun to question all of the things he had known, and therein seeing the fruit of his loins in his first born sons. After his release he stood upon the altar in the midst of the town and preached the gospel of the kingdom of The Creator.

But Semjaza rebuked him saying: "Oh son of man, who are you to speak to us with any words at all? For it was because of your sin that these are made and that all are here in this city. Are you more wise than we are? Wiser than the hosts of heaven? Are you wiser than the council of elohim? Stronger than Michael the Malakim of the throne? Are you as sturdy as the Ophanim who hold up the throne? Who are you, son of man, that The Creator is mindful of you? Don't you know that you were created lower than all the angels? For you are not like us, bene-elohim, for the only thing you are is like the ha-Satan, able to know good from evil. But that we already know as well. So then you only share the smallest part with us, foolish mud-man. Where is your rib? Why have you left her to be tempted by yet another serpent? Why are you here and why do you desire to say things to us? For you have your Councilor, but we are their councilors. You are of another world. We are of this world, the world outside the garden. You are not the true king."

And the people murmured against the king, siding with Semjaza.

But the king said to the Watchers: "Do you believe that under you will all the children of the earth become righteous? Under you will all the people offer adoration to The Creator? But there will come a day when they shall praise Him, and all shall worship Him. And the earth shall be cleansed from all defilement, and from all sin, and from all punishment, and from all torment, and He will never again send you upon the earth from generation to generation and forever. And in those days He will open the store chambers of blessing which are in the heaven, so as to send good Melach down upon the earth over the work and labor of the children of the earth and of the garden. And truth and peace shall be joined together throughout all the days of the world and throughout all the generations of men."

Then Azazel spoke and said: "You and your precious garden cave, full of wealth of all living kind that creeps and of all plant kind. But you have no heir. You left that place of solitude and serenity to dwell here? With the heir of shame? What a fool you are and what a fool you have always been. For all know that you did not eat of The Tree of Life, desirous of only knowledge. And how you left your rib and strode with animals to name them while she was free to be charmed by Leviathan. And how you have fallen, son of the morning star… Straight into The Land of Nod."

Then Semjaza's bastard sons, the Nephilim Hiwwa and Hiyya came to the south gate and roared but did not enter, for they were 19 cubits and 17 cubits tall and the men and woman all roared at the king to come down off the altar to Semjaza, but he would not, and a wind blew out of him, and he sang:

THE PSALM OF THE KING

"It is good to give thanks in the presence
Of Hashem Adonai El-Elyon Yehuah!
To praise Your name, Oh Most High, Yehuah.
To recount Your goodness in the morning,
And Your truth in the nights,
For You have made me glad,
Hashem Adonai El-Elyon, by Your works!
I will rejoice in the works of Your hands, Yehuah.
How great are your works, Hashem Adonai El-Elyon;
Your thoughts are very deep!
A foolish son of earth will not know it,
And a fool will not comprehend this.
While the wicked flourish like grass
And all workers of deceit blossom!
He is going to destroy them forever, even Yehuah.
Yes You are high and supreme in this age
Hashem Adonai El-Elyon!
And You are high and supreme in the age to come.
And You, your hand is supreme
To punish the wicked in the age to come!
Even in the great day of judgment, Oh Yehuah!
Your hand is supreme to give a good reward
To the righteous in the age to come
Oh Hashem Adonai El-Elyon.
Behold Your enemies Hashem Adonai El-Elyon!

Behold, Your enemies will perish in the age to come!
All the workers of deceit will be separated
From the band of the righteous.
Yahuah, You have raised up my might like a wild-ox!
You have anointed me with moist anointing oil of the leafy olive.
And my eye has looked on the perdition of my oppressors!
My ear has heard the sound of the destruction
Of those who stand against me to do harm.
The righteous man will grow fruit like the palm-tree!
Like the cedar in Lebanon he will grow and produce roots.
His sons will be planted in the sanctuary
Of Hashem Adonai El-Elyon!
In the court of the house of our Adonai they will flourish.
Again like their fathers they will produce sons in old age!
They will be plump and juicy.
So that the inhabitants of the earth might tell it!
For Hashem Adonai El-Elyon is upright.
Yehuah is my strength and there is no wrong in Him
Or in The Word of Yehuah."

LAMACH GUARDS THE KING

And the Watchers were sore afraid of the song, for in it was a prophesy against them and it spoke the name of The Creator, the name that they were not allowed to speak, should their tongues be ripped from their mouths by the Metatron, who stood watch over their mouths so they should not speak His name. And the Metatron is The Word, who sits at the right hand of The Creator and does all things by Him, for by Him was all things made, and through Him all things were made, naught was made that was made.

At this, Hiwwa and Hiyya threw the gate down to the ground and strode in to kill the king. But Semjaza stopped them, holding his hands aloft, whispering the tongues of the Malach to them, as they were but dumb beasts. And their eyes dimmed, losing their clarity and they stopped their conspiracy and slopped away, back to the plains. Seeing this was an opportune time, I told my three sons to grab the king off of the altar and bring him with us.

And he came down from the altar as though a dead man, as though he had been struck blind. Therefore as he could not move on his own, Tubal-Cain carried him alone into my tent, where I had first met him, when he had come to me. And the town glowered after us and I thought they might perform upon us the sin of Cain. Though the king would not wake, I could not see to release him back to the people of the city or to the Watchers for it was to me an inner knowledge that they would perform the sin of the Watchers against him.

And I bade my sons follow me and I commanded my wives Adah and Zillah and my daughter, Tubal-Cain's sister Nammah, to tend for him until our return. I bade them to fasten him together, as one might do a wild boar, with his hands and feet bound as one, with metalwork shackles, the same that Tubal-Cain had made, as they had been the same shackles used on him in his house. We bound him hand and foot in his sleep and he did moan and his eyes rolled back in his head but he showed no sign beyond that of being within the realm of our presence.

My wives and daughters were to stay with the king until we returned and that nothing evil should befall him, for in the protection of the king against the sin of Cain, I would serve for myself a marker for good to The Creator, so that I might perchance win a spot at the right hand of the king. The king would be in protection from himself and all the men outside who might hurt him. And the giants, though they would rip my tent asunder should they be allowed, had not been allowed by their father, the wayward Watcher, who did not want the death of the king of the garden on his hands.

LAMACH GOES TO MEET CAIN

And we went out to the field where Cain lived to talk with him and find out whether it was good to let the men of the city do the sin of Cain upon him or to release him to roam where he would or if we should bind him forever or cast him into utter darkness of Dudael where there would be the great gnashing of bones. For we were sore vexed within our deepest parts that we thought we would die. For in this life, the iniquities of the father are visited upon the children of those who hate them, but mercy is shown unto thousands, to those who know life and keep the commands of love.

When we did not find Cain at his field, we found his wife at their house, for Cain refused to live in the city he had built for his son. Themech, whose name was Awan, was there and bade us enter into the home and also into her. But we feared Cain so we stayed outside and built a little hut to sleep in for the night but Cain came to the home just as we had made a fire to eat goat flesh with, for we had killed one of his goats to eat. And it was a sacrificial goat, the one that goes away to Azazel, for it was black of color and of horn and its eyes and hooves were black with the sin of the people. And the goat was with nanny, also black of color, so we took the kid, killing her, for we were sore hungry and we milked the nanny and boiled the kid in its mother's milk, as a testament to Azazel that we would honor his sacrifice.

He stood at our fire for some time working long stalks of grain into a hoop, very beautiful of appearance while we told all of what happened in the city and that we wished to talk to him of these matters and what to do with the king, his father. But behind his eyes there was a roaring fire and he strode away and said simply: "Morning," meaning that we would discuss these dire events the next day. We dared not tell him of his wife's invitation for the fear of his wrath.

Then he took the hoop of grasses and looked up to heaven and mouthed words we could not understand and threw the hoop into the fire, under our kettle. It burned as all grass burns and at this his face remain unchanged, though tears came down his face at the still silence of the night. He sat with us, and ate some of the meat, then dismantled our spit and placed the rest of the kid in the fire with fresh wood and watched it burn down with us.

Jabal asked: "Why sacrifice to them if you do not serve them?" I thought to box him on the head but Cain stayed my hand.

"It is a question I have asked myself as well. And I have only to answer you that while The Creator has given me the breath I have, all the good things that I crave were given me by His Watchers. Besides my breath, The Creator only gives toil."

Cain stared long into the fire and was silent. And we pondered these things. He sat with us for some time, eyes closed, until a screech owl called, seeming to snap him out of his reverie. He opened his eyes, and seeing the kid was burned away, he kicked out our fire and said: "In the morning."

And so we slept.

LAMECH'S VISION

And a night vision came to me, and so it was that I found myself before a great wheeled beast with fire and feathers and eyes came to me and he caught me up and led me far toward the sides of the north and westward past Eden to the distant mountain of Bashan, and the Spirit of The Creator was not there and I was dead afraid. And it was not yet my time, but only the time where Cain had been cast away from The Head of Days, The Lord of Spirits, from the garden. And no one but I could see the great wheeled beast and we arrived in the midst of a meeting of more than 13 score of Archons, as well as many others. And there I beheld them in secret.

Before me were the seven head Apkallu and their ten Archons and before them were The Watchers and seven great Apkallu pleaded with them to give up their quest with the women of the children of the earth. And Semjaza was there, seducing them with the mantle of the ha-Satan upon him and he was saying…

"…And I alone will not bear the penalty for the deed, for if it be a sin, then why did The Creator deem us to desire them if we should not desire them? And they walk here and there, to and fro naked. If they did not want to be taken, then why would they be thus? For we have planned this thing and we shall do it. There exists for us many for each of us to take, but it is good that we should only take one until such a time as we may take whatever we desire, for indeed, the whole of creation shall subject to our seed."

But The Seventy Princes left them then, chastising and chiding them for their actions. Michael, the Prince of Yis-Ra-El chided them saying: "Yahuah rebuke you." And many left, but the Princes of

Magog and Tarshish remained with their horde, to see what would be said.

And there remained 12 Thrones that were not Watchers nor Princes but they were set apart. And one named Uruk had black elephant tusks sewn into his mantle. And they heeded not the Watchers nor the Princes, but were like the Princes in nature but not Princes. And their names were Kish, and Ur, Sippar, Akshak, Karak, Nippur, Adab, Umma, Lagash, Tiberia, Larsa, and Uruk was among them, their chief.

Then Azazel spoke to the ten score Archons saying: "It is indeed a great sin that we shall commit, therefore let us find in all the earth, all of the men of the earth and seduce them there. It comes to me that we should scour every dry land portion and deep place so that should there come a punishment, The Creator cannot find and punish all of us and our seed will remain with man forever. It comes to me that we should fly towards the garden and to the sides of the north as well as to the four ends. There are, by chance, children of earth who dwell with the four great Malach who hold back the winds, at their feet. And they are hidden from all who seek them, and to them some of us should remain."

And Semjaza said: "I will take the strongest of you with me, then near to where the men of the garden are, for it is in my mind that his rib is the most comely of all the sons of the hadam, though she be not one."

But the earth shook, and from the heaven came a great beast, like unto a sea serpent with wings, and it flew over us and then landed among them with a terrible thunder.

"No." It said. "For she is mine."

Then I was suddenly with my sons in our tent, covered in a dense sweat. And I kept this within me, not knowing what it could mean.

CAIN SPEAKS

The next day we awoke to a distinct smell coming from outside the hut. I did not forget my vision in the night but resolved to not speak of it before Cain and only to ponder what it could mean.

We rose and found Cain already preparing breakfast of Sowback and barleymeal. He stripped long pieces of sowback onto a spit and roasted them before dropping them whole into the barley. The smell was overpowering and we ate straightway with our hands from wooden bowls.

"Youth today sleep too long." He grumbled as he ate as well. He had a carved stick with three prongs on one end. Jabal marveled at the device, asked to see it, and Cain gave it to him, pulled out another, and continued to eat. After a short while, Cain began to clean up the site and asked the others to dismantle the tent and make the ground as it was. After this was done, the fire was rekindled and Cain came back out to them and sat on the ground, expectantly. I cleared my throat, not knowing what to say.

"Did you enter into my wife?" Cain asked, without provocation.

Assuring him that this was not so, he waved his hand. "I would have smelled her on you. I know you did not. Otherwise, I would sin again and the guilt would be on your heads." He eyed us one by one. "You are the seventh in the line from me. Yet I see that you and your children bear my mark. They are fresh, but how did this come to be?

And why did you shear your hair? I recall Jabal had such wondrous locks. No, do not tell me for I already know the answer to this as well. The dead boy at the altar was your doing, and you are claiming a ten time portion for yourself from my mark to yourselves. I do not think this will be the case, as the mark I bear was written by The Word. For He came to me, from the voice of The Creator… The Adam's Creator. His Word came and touched my hand and my head and pronounced upon me the mark's curse."

We eyed him, surprised at this.

"Oh? You think this is a blessing?" He pointed to his turban and then to the cloth that bound his wrist. "You think I enjoy being the one who such a sin is named after? When I go to bathe in the river, I see the mark in the stillness of the pool. When I lay with my wife or my daughters, there is the mark on my hand. When I slay the wild-men, there is the mark. When I work with the grain, there is the mark."

"In all of my contention and striving after my younger brother, I did not become the blessed one. In all of my groaning to do after the heart of The Creator, He did not find my sacrifice worthy, so I killed him that was in the way and so now I must bear the consequence. No one has followed my sin except for the wild men of the earth, but they are not men of the garden and they are not of us. Slaughtering a man of the earth is like unto slaughtering this boar that we fed upon. Meat from the wild-men and meat from the boar give us strength. One day I plan on eating a man of the sons of the garden. Maybe I will eat my father. The time is not for that yet. Maybe I will kill and eat one of you."

"But you are not here to talk about the son of the king, because you seek to know what to do with the king. Release him to the Watchers or the men of the city or to do whatsoever he wilt on his own? I know these are your questions. I tell you that I do not know, but there is a bene-elohim that knows and he is not a Watcher, but an Archon, a Prince. The chief of this place, though I do not know why he has not come yet. In truth, I pray he never comes so that I will remain here, in the ways that I have chosen."

JUBAL'S GIFT

Tubal-Cain was toying with a small shard of metalwork around his neck while Cain was talking.

"What is it you have there?" Cain asked.

Tubal-Cain smiled and brought it up. "Jubal helped me build it. It produces a birdsong when blown," he said and blew on it. It was two bright metalwork leaves, closely bound together. He held it a finger width away from his mouth and blew softly. "Reeeeeee!" It sang. Cain's eyes were wide and snatched it out of his hand, brought it to his mouth and blew. Nothing.

Tubal-Cain said, "Try a little closer."

Cain blew and a gentle *Reeeee!* came forth from the bright metalwork. It was on a strip of leather, so he slipped it around his neck. Tubal-Cain opened his mouth to say something and Cain silenced him with a "What?" for he had not guessed the gift was his but had taken it even so. He eyed Tubal-Cain to challenge him. Jabal handed him the pronged eating stick and looked at Tubal-Cain, smiling. Cain pretended to not notice this. Only Jubal had a distant look in his eyes, not looking at Cain, fearing what he would say.

"We shall journey. We will take what you have with us then. We will start today, for it is yet early. We must seek out the Prince of the land far towards the sides of the north and on his mountain. It is a far walk, we will follow the Tigris toward the sides of the north from Babylon and there we will climb. Where the Tigris and Euphrates depart as friends, there I have built another city. We will travel until we find your Prince."

"What is Babylon, my father?" I asked.

He laughed. "And you think I only farm? Do you think Enoch is the only city that I have built? Indeed, we may find others along the way. Strike your camp, for the day is not as long as you would want."

Cain departed, going to the house for his things. And Themech ran out to us as we were departing and gave us several breads, fruits, and meats for our journey. She offered herself to us again, but we were determined to be on the way. And if Cain had not deterred us before, knowing that he desired man-flesh to eat deterred us even further.

When Cain returned, he had fashioned a cloth purse upon his back with long rods, and it carried all that he needed.

PAST BABYLON

Finding Babylon was just as he said, and we did pass several other peoples. Some were along the Tigris, but many far away, near smaller streams afraid to come near us as we walked close to the water. We walked with a swiftness double the speed of the men of the earth, for we had the blood of the Adam and were not mere hadam of their blood. They were afraid of us, but at Babylon we saw signs of other men of the garden and we realized they must be of

Cain, but then we also saw many other shapes and figures there, as well as Watchers.

One, named Armaros, who some called Marduk, detained us, and he rode on the back of a terrible lizard, as a steed. He galloped towards us and feigned hatred, but when he saw Cain, he got off his mount and bowed low in respect to the man of the garden under the rule of Semjaza. Then he let us pass. We knew not whose offspring the lizard was, but it had to have been his own, for there were others in similar appearance and there were only what appeared to be 10 Watchers here as well as men of the garden and of the earth that were of Cain's son Olad. We were given food but were not allowed to stay in the city after nightfall, and remained outside the city walls, camped at the gate.

Cain, however, stayed in the city.

In the night we saw what could not be described, but Jubal was the first to wake. On the horizon, walking as men, were a troupe of men the shape and size of hills, the height of which was six threescore and six cubits. They moved slowly, walking along the western edge of the Tigris. The ground rumbled as they passed. They were naked and only one of them had manhood, but they were all men. There were seven of them, six of them being gilded. No clothes they wore, but on the top of the head of the mountain sized man was a covering that looked to be a vessel used on the seas.

PRINCE URUK OF THE MOUNTAIN

We arrived finally at the base of the mountain where we would find Prince Uruk on the peak. We traveled the day and on the next morning we came to his abode near the summit. There he sat on a black ivory throne, looking down at us, and beyond.

"Sons of the garden, why have you come here? Don't you know my time is not yet? For it is alloted to me to rule your kind for a time, time, and half a time and that time is not now, nor will it be until the time is come. So, I ask you, why have you come to my silver mountain abode? Is it to ask for a boon from your future Prince, for in truth, I cannot give you a boon until I have been given power over you. And, as you know, you are marked from All-Father with the mark you bear, for you have broken one of the great commands of the ages."

Unsure of what to say to all of this, Cain bowed low and said: "My lord and my master. We have taken my father, the man from the garden into our possession. And we know that if The Creator finds us, He may punish us. And the punishment I endure is more than I can endure already. Give us wisdom on what to do with my father, for if we release him, he will tell The Creator and punish us all the more."

"Ask your current Prince what to do." Uruk mocked.

But Cain responded, "Nay, they are interlopers, breeding with us, taking our women, making monstrous creatures of their own and teaching us worthless mysteries. They are but for a time and a season, this you and I know, for you are the inheritor of the great land and city of Enoch, and his sons. We are your inheritance and we seek your wisdom on this."

"Fools and small minded men. If you four are the hope of man then my punishment for my transgression is worse than he intends to punish me for my eventual rebellion against Him. For in truth, I am finding my pre-punishment much more than I can bear, but I cannot do anything because if I rebel now, will I be allowed to rule anything? Or shall I practice the sin of Cain upon you and force your generations to start again? Shall The All-Father start again with another batch of hadam and another of the Adam with another garden? Or are you a test from The All-Father to see what I shall do? Tell me truthfully, are you from Him or are you from yourselves on your own behalf? Do you really have the Adam? Tell me."

At this, all four trembled in fear and Cain shouted: "If I told you anything, I would be lying." Cain said, gesturing to me. "For we have concocted this plan without provocation. It was Lamach who intended to do him injustice while I desired to speak with you before any sin was committed against him. For it is the seventh born from me who tells this tale. He says he took him, and I, like a fool, believed him. Now, I am of a mind to agree with you, great Prince. For his foolishness and treachery are beyond me."

Cain, betraying me before this Prince, greatly angered me and I responded. "No!"

I stood and took a step forward towards the great Prince on this throne. "It is the truth that we have captured him. He was held captive at Enoch, the first city of Cain, by the people of the city for they desired a king but did not desire what he had to say. There they held him until he provoked them and so we took him and kept him, for he was not himself. And we wish to be rid of him and of The Watchers. But they are too many, and they take all of our women, and make us into things they desire so that we are no longer men. If they are allowed to do these things, we will no longer be the men you desire to rule, because they will have devoured us all."

PRINCE URUK SPEAKS

At this, Prince Uruk had risen from his throne and stood above us, shouting. He was not angry at us, but at the city.

"They desired a king?" He stamped his foot and the mountain shook. "But do they not understand that I shall soon become their king? I feel that I may not rule even unto the ten score Nanna until I am allotted to take charge fully over all of the kingdoms of these lands." He was furious.

"My god," started Cain, "Men are not, as yet, old enough on the earth to flourish until the end of your reign, for even the man of the garden is yet five score. Help us rid ourselves of the false Prince Semjaza and his cohort Azazel so that we might be the people you may yet rule."

"You would not even need me had your father forsaken the garden. The All-Father had Eden build a house of loaves and fish for all nations, and His Word and His Spirit did desire to sup with all men in that place for all generations. But your father took what The All-Father made and discarded it, believing the old dragon in the place. He trusted that which he did not understand. For that which the Hand of He who made the great bowl above you shall surely curse you all the while under the bowl you remain. You will be cursed in the city and cursed in the country. Even your kneading troughs and collecting bushels will be cursed, and though it will be a large stone around your neck, yes even the bowels of your daughters will bring forth strange flesh. Like metalwork that should be discarded or still-birthed, are you cursed beyond all the creatures of the earth."

Cain, I, and my three children were silent at this. For we knew not what to say, or even if we should say anything. I chewed the inside of my lip for some time.

"Kiss the dirt of the lord you serve." The Prince said, finally.

And we bowed low and kissed the dirt before him. And we were silent then until he made his proclamation.

Then he said to us: "Thus it was given me to give charge over your kind after a fashion for a time, but the time is not yet, so the words I would say to you would be to let the Adam go and let him return to his rib, for The All-Father has plans for him yet, and His ways are not our ways, and His thoughts are not our thoughts. But as for you and your problem of evil in your midst, I have naught for you. For you are evil from the beginning Cain, you are of your father, the evil one. This much I know to be true, that all four of you are workers of iniquity. Yes, even you Lamach, for you sit idle while others rape around you, doing nothing, carving this sortid tale upon the tablets. Yes, you Jabal, for you sew as much discord as you sew in skin. You Jubal, for you make instruments of pleasure and they are used in proclamation in all vain festivals, and especially you, Tubal-Cain. You are like your forefather in deed and in name, yet are the more crafty about it, for you swear to do right but stab others on their backside with the very blades you forge for them. You are all evil and it is my penance to even have you before my face. You stink of the fires of Sheol beneath and I rue the day I must come to you. Now. I have said my peace. Begone from me."

"But Prince! What of our plight!?" Exclaimed Tubal-Cain.

"Bah. Go to Nineveh. The All-Father will appear to you on the way. For even now He knows my mind, but His grace is sufficient for me."

THE OPHANIM

Cain knew of Nineveh yet had never been there. I asked how that could be and it was told to me to not ask such questions. Eventually I understood. For, though we never got to Nineveh, we encountered its people along the way. They were tall and tan of skin with the wide brows of the men of the earth and they were powerful in stature, half a cubit taller than the men of the earth where we lived. And as we walked by them, we stayed to our own side of the Tigris, for there it was in two branches and smaller. And The Creator had plans for us that were not the plans of our Prince, for at the river we beheld a mystery.

And as we came to a strangely bright forested spot. Then the sky darkened and there were seven thunders in the sky, and there was suddenly darkness and before us. Then there appeared a great light, like the circle wheel from my dream and it came before us. It was the same wheel within a wheel covered in feathers, eyes, and flames as I had seen before; it stood in our way.

That wheel which was called an Ophanim uncoiled itself in front of the bright forest, and behind it was a vastly even brighter forest, about the color as the forests I knew for the brief times as they were before the winter. But these trees stood before me as gold and scarlet and bright violets such as I had never seen before and while the Ophanim was still uncoiling a figure of a man came up from the trees, suddenly, as if he were taking one stride in his gait but moving at the speed of ten gaits. And it was the red wanderer, the planet who presides over death, the restrainer. And he strode to us as if in haste, but when he approached it was again the sound of seven thunders uttering rushing waters and the visage was of a dark cloud.

"Behold the vast house of the world, and behold a great wind shall sweep across it. And the four Archons who stand holding it back shall hold it back no longer. And it will come to pass that they who deceive will come out to deceive many, and the great Malach will not be able to hold them back. But at that time, He will lift up a standard for all the nations and assemble the banished ones, and he will gather the dispersed from the four corners of the earth. But lo! Son of perdition. Are you here before me now to stand in my way, or to stand to the side and let the judgment on the houses commence? Will you be in the way of the restrainer and become chuffa under the plow? What will you, oh wayward son of the king?"

And slowly the black cloud cleared and I beheld the vision of the great black-red robed Archon, with a reaper's curved blade. And Cain knew the tool for Tubal had made him one. But the Archon's was covered in the blood of the sons of the Watchers.

"Who brings the houses of snow and hail, which are reserved for the great time of trouble? Who are they that direct the sky swords, or pushes back against the eastern winds? Who shall carve the sluice for the great time, or clear the path for the sky hammer to bring the gates down upon the barren places? To satisfy Dudael? To make the land sprout with tender shoots. Do the gate waters hold back without permission from The I AM? Who brings breath to the mountain dew? Who births the ice on the wall? Can you tame the tongues of Kimath or bind the tzits of Kasil? Can you bring the Mazzaroth? Can you tame Ayish and her sons?"

SAMAEL APPEARS

And before an answer could be made to him by me or my sons, Cain stood up and said: "I am the first born man and I know how The Creator commands you to instruct us thus. But let us pass, for in this place it was given to us to understand that we might gain wisdom on how to seduce away Semjaza and Azazel from our midst, so that we might rule over the people there instead of them who would rule over us. For they have bewitched my people and taught them strange magic and his metalwork is more cunning than all. For he and Semjaza have given us gifts that we might come closer to them, and it has made us closer to them but also more needy of them. The more they make us manumitted, the more they lead us into vassalage."

Samael inhaled a large breath and proclaimed, "Verily but that ye know that The I AM is the ruler upon all the earth and that His house is without end ye therefore may be given a way of escape, and the escape is not for thee to have but it shall unto thee a contagonist against the workings of evil men and of The Watchers and over all their tools, weapons, and designs of evil."

For in all the giving of gifts we forgot to receive them without snare. For in all of our getting, we forgot to get wisdom. For in the getting of the things that made us beholden more to ourselves, it entangled us to become reliant upon them all the more. For if the right hand gives a knife, in the left there is yet another.

Samael continued, "But if ye wish to be rid of Azazel and his cohorts who teach thee these things and defile thy women then this shalt thou do. Verily build an altar to The I AM. Then shalt thou lay both hands on a pure and spotless white goat and do lay both hands on its head and confess thy iniquity and rebellious acts and place all sin and idolatry upon its head. Then shalt thou worship The I AM who made the morning stars and the morning stars shall flee from thee. Take and send the goat away into the wilderness by thy own hand, oh Cain. Then shalt the goat carry on itself all the iniquities into Dudael. Then thou shall have peace from them, for in that day, The I AM will send a way of escape for thee and the iniquity laid upon thine household shall come to an end."

But this made Cain sad, for this was the way in which Abel had given an acceptable sacrifice unto The Creator and Cain had rebelled against it then. But something in the way Cain looked at him, I knew the sacrifice would be taken with the sincerity it was meant.

Then Cain said: "Therefore I will bear upon my oppressors the iniquity laid upon me. He shall make their land into dust and powder. It will descend on them from the sky until they are destroyed. They will be plagued with curses and confusion and rebuke all that they have given us. They will have boils and scabs on their heads and knees and thighs. They will have madness, blindness, and confusion. Then The Word and king of the garden and the whole of the earth will give them over to other sons of God and they will not harvest where they have planted. The locust and cankerworm will consume all they have sown. For they are like trees, planted by the rivers of the dead. Their leaves will wither and whatsoever they do will not prosper. They will be like the chaff, which the wind drives away. The heat of the day will consume them and they will have no shade."

THE CREATURES

Then Samael left just as he had come, and the Ophanim coiled again and the land grew dark from behind it, within the forest behind it.

And it spoke, saying: "The guardians of Tartarus encamp around those who fear him and deliver them, for behold, The Spirit of Power commanded the Red Planet Samael to send them to the earth. Behold, I am sending creatures ahead of you to guard you along the way and bring you to the place He has prepared. They shall guard those who dare try their escape from their immutable future. They are not the brood of The Watchers for they are beyond the touch of their kind. But they are of Tartarus itself, meant to restrain The Watcher's brood when the time comes. And they shall be to your borders, as in like a cliff. And wherever they go, no one else will go, lest the guardians tear them asunder. They carry with them the smell of the very pit and their speech is that of all the underworld. No one who seeks them returns. And those who see them are not believed."

And from the forest came beasts like the wild-men, the men of the earth that The Creator had first prepared, but they were not like the men. Nor were they like the children of The Watchers, nor were they like The Watchers. They were a force of the earth, a force of the uncreated power of The Word and a force from the land itself. They walked towards us in shaggy unkempt strides, like men who bore a heavy load. There was an army of them and they wandered towards us but stayed away in the trees, so as to not be seen. From where the great Ophanim was we saw that the forest was dotted here and there with eyes like the eyes of a hungry animal, but we knew they were not animals.

And from within and behind the wheel of the Ophanim there came a sound and a smell, so strong was it that Jubal ran violently down towards the river, falling along the way, as if stricken with madness. Tubal-Cain grabbed a hold of me, shaking me.

"We must run from this place, father!" He cried out and spat blood.

Jabal and myself remained as if in a trance and Cain stood, feet wide, clenching his knife.

Then the Ophanim spoke to them saying: "Behold, a day is coming, burning like a furnace, when all the evildoer will be stubble, for they shall be set ablaze. But to those who fear the name of The Word, Shemesh Sadach will rise with healing in his wings. Then you shall trample the wicked for they are ashes under the soles of your feet. For The Name of The Word is a strong tower, a refuge in time of trouble."

Then a high shriek emitted from the shaggy men that continued on for some time and I was undone, relieving my bowels where I stood. Jabal had done the same.

Then he spoke unto us saying: "Behold, the coming of the awesome Great Day of The Creator comes, as with wings on the wind."

Thus, he closed himself up like a sunset and he disappeared from the place. The vision of the eternal forest receded and the great beasts faded from view. Still, their smell lingered, as the smell of Tartarus and Sheol might. For they were not beasts given to Cain to defend against the wiles of The Watchers. They were beasts given to the earth to defend itself. Cain did not move as of yet, but sank to his knees after a time. Jubal came back to us and we sat with Cain for a while, not knowing what else to do. Tubal-Cain took off his bear skin mantle and wrapped it over Cain's shoulders. We were still for a while then heard footsteps of The Prince of Uruk coming towards us. His great purple robes with black elephant tusks interwoven, whipped in the wind and his feet were shod in frost.

PRINCE URUK REACTS

And The Prince prophesied saying: "A new creature on the earth he sends to thee. For in truth, my kind had not foreseen this. For since the days of creation we held not our peace, but He instead gave them to us. As though blind, we saw through the light of Him. Though deaf, we heard through the voice of Him. For The Spirits of The Creator of all are just and kind and good and they seek ever the indwelling. And He sent His Word and healed men's disease. His Word is a light to the feet and a light along the path. How then do we keep the path of purity? By living according to The Word. Blessed are they that hear The Word and endure it and obey it. For as grass withers and flowers fail, The Word endures forever. The man who hears The Word and puts it into practice is like a man who builds his house upon a rock. For Heaven and earth shall pass away, but The Word will remain forever."

But Cain said: "HIs Word is a torment to my soul. For His Word walked with my father in the garden, but because of Leviathan, he was cast out."

Prince Uruk rebuked him. "It was not Leviathan nor The Dragon who sinned. For they have been sinning from the beginning. But the woman, who gave the fruit from the tree of knowledge, gave it to the man to eat. They were in sin. For the Adam was meant for wisdom, not knowledge. Knowledge by itself brings grief and sin. Wisdom first brings hope and life. When knowledge is born, then lust is conceived. This gives birth to sin, and sin brings death. Look at the good you and your sons have gotten from the mysteries these Watchers have given you. The payment of sin is death. And death shall reign over you. Even those who did not sin like the Adam, since the sin is here, death still reigns. So. What benefit do you derive from those things that you are now ashamed of? They all result in death. But fear not. For by The Word, all will find life. For anyone who calls on The Name of The Word shall be saved."

And I said to him: "You have opened my eyes, as well as the eyes of my family. Better is one day outside the house of my god than a thousand anywhere else. I would rather be a guard at your door than dwell in the tent of the wicked."

"You fool and blind. I am not your god, nor ever shall be." He said and turned away.

And since it was dark, we slept where we lay.

TRAVELING TO THE CITY

In the time of our troubles, in the other world, on the mountain, we had not thought about the safety of the first man, for our minds were continually aware of the presence of the guardians of Tartarus behind us wandering in and out of the forests. A great multitude had followed us, traveling south, ever out of range but the terror of their smell lingered. Great shaggy men following when we walked and slowing when we stopped... By night of our third day walking south, many had gone around us to the forests where they might settle. But one of them, a large red haired beast, easily 6 cubits tall, followed us without remorse, without hiding. It was a distinct smell it had and we grew accustomed to it, and it bothered us no more. It was but one of thousands.

On the morning of our fourth day traveling south, we came to a small city which we knew not. There were no men of Cain there but Cain walked to them and greeted them, and they were all sons of earth. They smelled us and a great fear overcame them and they bowed and worshiped Cain. He met with the largest of them and went into one of their small tents. After a while, a call went out and many of the young women came to the tent. We camped a way off, but the people of the town beckoned us to join them. My sons did so but I did not, fearing that someone would take our belongings so I stayed at the camp alone not interfering in the sins of Cain. In the morning I was still alone. Jubal, Jabal and Tubal having stayed with Cain in the tents of the people. Of the red haired guardian there was no sign. The smell of women was on all of the men. I spat in disgust until Cain slapped me in the back of the thigh laughing and handed me some roasted lamb.

"Eat, dour face." He chided. "Not all of us have two wives." And laughed. My sons laughed with him, mocking me.

But I was resolute in my belief that there must be a way to find salvation through my actions. For there is a god who is The Creator of gods and He has made all of this for some reason. Though I did not know what it was, surely there was more than: "Be fruitful and multiply, fill the earth and subdue it." I would ask the king upon my return if there was a way for salvation for me or my kind or if I should give in to the life Cain led. For the hopes of all men are dashed where there is no love. The schemes of all are brought low by the situations that crash around them, such as they did I and my sons, and the father of us all, when we came back to the city.

WE RETURN

In our absence, our imprisonment of the king had become the chief totem of a festival that the whole of the city was enjoying. For in the absence of Cain, there had been only the law of Semjaza and Azazel and The rest of The Watcher kind. Enoch cared not, nor Irad, nor any of the forefathers, nor men, about who ruled the town in the absence of strong men like myself or my son Tubal. Women from all the land had come and were striving to become impregnated with the seed of the king, though he was not able to escape to save himself. They had fermented barleymeal and the fruit of the vine and continuously gave him eat and drink of it and he did not know himself. Cain's wife and my wives and daughters were chief among them who sought to lay with him, for they were holding him hostage but he knew it not.

But the steadfast love of The Creator is unceasing and though many women tried mounting the king, his seed remained in him and did not spill on the ground, nor go into another. And the king's member remained unwavering in its limber, so that even the comeliest creature elicited no reaction from the king.

This was at Cain's tent, for in our time away, my wives had moved our tents and all that we had into Cain's fields and there was a sight of dread on Cain's face when he beheld the waste before us. Trampled were the vineyards and the grains and all of the vegetables had been laid waste by the brood of the Watchers. The pressing mills, the threshing floors were all torn down and in their place was remnants of great bonfires. There were fruit trees that had been felled and of the storage tents, they were burned as well. In places, we could still see the sacrificial pikes where they burned their effigies and fetishes to The Watchers. Among them were children, also having been sacrificed to the ilk of the sinful ones.

It was yet early in the morning, for we had traveled mid-night until the Shemesh made its first rays known on the land. It had been one fortnight that we had traveled to the silver mountain and it was Sabbath early in the day where we found ourselves at the Irad gate again. They were wide open, not having been shut the day before.

Hiwwa and Hiyya slept there, dead in their drunken dreams until Cain stood on top of Hiwwa and grabbed his neck like one does a dog.

"Why are the gates to my city open!?" He demanded, at which Hiwwa and Hiyya both roused and began to draw up weapons to fight.

"Doth thou seek to entreat with thy mouth or thy sword?" He shouted, and, drawing his small blade, drove it deep into the neck of Hiwwa until the giant drowned in his own blood. HIyya stood aghast at his brother dying before him until my three sons dragged him down, gouged out his eyes and did the same to his neck.

Cain, having climbed upon the body of Hiwwa, drew out the whistle from around his neck and blew into it with a great force.

We heard, as if in answer, a whistling off in the distance and the red giant and a hundred others of his height came shambling and running towards us with great force, and burst around us as water does down a hillside, and there was among them, an even larger brute still, as white as Nanna herself.

WAR ON THE WATCHERS

Swift was the hand of the fierce guardians upon the city of Enoch, for it was as if the underworld had been released upon it and the Watchers and their brood were driven as a locust swarm before a storm. The high *kreening* of the guardians and their terrible stench washed over the city so that the people of the city could not move as the terrible clawed hands of the guardians swept over those who were bastards, removing their throats in one swooping movement and onto the next. Half breeds twice their size stood no chance before their brute knotted arms and teeth. Blades danced and met with fur and though many were slain thus, the numbers of the guardians of Tartarus was unrelenting.

The large red beast stood atop the rubble of Adam's house and opened his mouth, to not roar but rather something akin to a growl that made the stomach turn into knots. It made all who heard it stumble and fall. And the men of garden and the men of the earth they touched not, for they only were slaying the giants, and the fallen ones, and the bastard spirits of the Watchers brood. So many who had one small part relation but who were otherwise friends of my family were cut down, stem to stern. And they were not cruel, but rather they did what no one could, but cleanse the city of the cruelty that had been transpiring since Cain's first woman gave birth and the Watchers had arrived to conquer the men with their metal, and the women with their ventrals.

For the guardians of the forest were seeming eunuchs, or rather they had not sex at all, but rather, had only rage. Their demeanor was a wave upon the rocks, they moved over their enemies until only sodden clumps remained. The complete destruction of the bastards was so complete it was only those who escaped were the ones who survived. And we who survived were condemned to remember only the faces of our family, the hands of our loved ones, for there were none left who were injured only, nor were there faces remaining. Like Samael the destroyer, they washed over the city with total vengeance.

We had not remembered just how many of us there were among us who were bastards, but when we looked at who remained we remembered. That my mother's sister had been taken by a Nephilim and that now this whole line was now cursed by The Creator. I was reminded of this as my kin lay dying around me.

Of Semjaza, Azazel, Baraqueel, Kokabel, and many others who were accustomed to be there, I know not what happened to them, but the entire Sabbath was given over to Khayrem, the devotion to destruction, as before the Creator, whose cherubs stood with fiery swords by the gates of the Garden of Eden still to this day. So all the fleeing sons of The Watchers fled the City of Enoch and made their way out to other places. None was left alive in the city.

PURSUIT OF THE WATCHERS

During the Khayrem there stood among the great beasts one beast, a cubit taller than the rest, even taller than the great red beast, and it was white as the snows of the mountain of Prince Uruk. But he was not of the brood of the Watchers, but was raised up against them. And there he took up a small tree and ripped it from the root and took it up as a weapon for itself. And it stood and raised its awful arms above its head and roared with a howl of scorn and of rage. As many of the giants and monstrous beasts were fleeing the white giant directed the others who were milling about the houses to give chase, and so they chased them.

And many of us gave chase as well, even after many days to Bashan, the dwelling of Prince Uruk, even to Dudael and the gates of Sheol. And there the giants were chased into the caverns of the deep and many fell therein. The Watchers brood were as gazelles but we ran as horses and still we did not see their company again, but came upon them many days later as the beasts from Sheol were carrying with them many heads of the Watchers brood as if trophies and bid us not to come near them.

So there we stayed for a day, lighting a little fire to recover. We drank much water, and found warmth, and dozed for the day. At the dawn of Shemesh on the following morning, many of us with our brazen knives and long knives were awakened by the great white beast and the rough red beast and they stood far away singing a strange and mournful tale among themselves. Leaving a large hill of heads and hands behind, they melted away into the mountains and forests, leaving only the smell of Sheol behind.

Those with me who had followed the great hairy beasts as they pursued the Watchers brood were astonished at the amount of heads left there, for there were eight times the amount that we had known, and we walked home to our city by the sea, Enoch, not understanding where the great beasts had corralled the other Watchers brood from, so we believed either they brought them from the forests around them, or herded them as they went, collecting more until they drove them into the abyss, by the foundations of the deep, at the pillars of the earth.

And so we took back to Enoch, this story, and the burning reminder in our noses.

LAMACH DECLARES THE CITY DESTROYED

The next day, while it was still yet dark, I climbed the west wall to survey the city below. I wept alone in the dark for what was lost, but still I felt as if the weight of a thousand stones had been lifted off of those of us that remained. It had been a week since the slaughter, and still so much carnage remained. Yet upon the walls were painted with their blood, glyphs of warning and signs that the city no longer would be bound by Semjaza and Azazel, the ha-Satans who devoured our people and pillaged our goodness.

As the sky turned from black to blue, fires began being lit here and there. Brass censers and lamp flames shown in some houses in and among the now ruined city. As the rays from Shemesh began to ignite the vault, the eastern sky gave fire to the blue, and when finally Shemesh appeared I stood and drew out a ram's horn that had been carved and had been with me my whole life, for it had been a gift to my father upon my birth.

And I blew it seventy times at the first sign of Shemesh. I blew until Shemesh had risen half cubit above the horizon and most of the City had come. Irad had come, his clothes tattered and his left arm missing but tightly bound up in fine cloth. He looked hale otherwise and they all gathered round. I addressed the people there and told them:

"We have returned from Bashan, towards the sides of the North, we have witnessed all manner of the brood of the filth that has held us captive for so long, vanquished before the mighty wave of the guardians of Tartarus. Of the king, I know not! Of Cain, I know not! Of Enoch, I know not! But of Irad, he stands here alive but mildly scratched. Of his sons and of the rest of your sons, I know not! What I do know is my sons are here! My wives are here! And that I shall find out about the remainder of the sons, daughters, wives, mothers, and fathers."

"Your fathers and mothers and sons and daughters that were impure have been cleansed from the land. And that is a work of The Creator and we shall indeed weep for them, but we know that we stand whole and pure as men of the garden and of the earth, without the strain of The Watchers upon our necks any longer. Though they have taken our loves from us with their poison, we know that we stand pure before The Creator once again. Today we choose to serve Him above all others."

"That Semjaza and Azazel have left us and we are alive in the light of the original creation. No, this is not the great garden of The Creator, but we shall have our own garden soon, without the poison of their ha-Satan's control over us. We are free, my people! Freedom has washed over us in blinding force! The resolute victory of the sons of the garden and the sons of the earth is here!"

And by this time, it appeared that the whole of the remnants of the city were there, but they were in no mood to hear of victory or serving The Creator, for no sooner had I finished addressing them than they hesitated, looking at me, aghast. One or two turned and started back to their houses until a rock hit me on the chest and soon many more came and they cried out at me saying: "The wrath of The Creator is upon us because of you!" and "You are to blame for our family's destruction!" and "Semjaza was a good god and would never harm us in this way!" And my sons were among those who hated me.

I cried aloud and railed against their foolishness but they would not hear me.

KING ADAM ADDRESSES THE CITY

But king Adam was still in the City. He had not been among us in the pursuit of the Watcher's brood, he had remained here. Upon hearing my shofar call, he had come to see what I might say. When he saw their violence upon me, he climbed the wall and addressed them as well. I had not seen him in his own mind since his last speech to the people.

"Why do you rage, and imagine the vain thing that you would be, under less of a yoke, with these demons standing on your necks? These kings of the earth set themselves and the rulers take counsel together, against Hashem Adonai El-Elyon, and against His anointed, saying, 'Let us break His bands asunder, and cast away their cords from us.' He that sits in the heavens laughs. Yahuah shall have them in derision. Then shall he speak unto them in his wrath, and vex them in his sore displeasure."

"Hashem Adonai El-Elyon, will vindicate His people and have compassion on His servants when He sees that their strength is gone! Even when no one remains, slave or free. Yahuah will say: 'Where are their gods, the rock in which they took refuge, which ate the fat of their sacrifices and drank the wine of their drink offerings? Let them rise up and help you; let them give you shelter!'"

"But they are gone and Yahuah has given you the city! His compassion is new and unyielding though you grew fat and kicked: becoming fat, bloated, and gorged. For you abandoned Hashem Adonai El-Elyon, who made you and you scorned the rock of your salvation. You provoked His jealousy with foreign gods and enraged Him with abominations. You sacrificed to demons, not to Hashem Adonai El-Elyon, but to the new gods you had not known, to the newly arrived gods, which your fathers did not fear."

"Behold El-Elyon! The cloud-rider El-Elyon! He rides on a cherub and flies hither; He came swiftly on the wings of the clouds! He made the clouds His chariot, walking on the wings of the wind. There is none like unto The Word of Yahuah who rideth upon the heaven to our aid, and His excellency is within the firmament. Behold, He rides on a swift cloud and comes to Eridu; and the

Nephilim will tremble at his presence, and the heart of the Watchers will melt within them."

"Behold!" He says: "I will take vengeance on My adversaries and repay those who hate Me. I will make My arrows drunk with blood, while My sword devours flesh of giants! The blood of the slain and captives, the heads of the enemy leaders."

"Rejoice, O heavens, with Him, and let all bene-elohim under and above the vault worship Him. Rejoice, oh nations, with His people; for He will avenge the blood of His children. He will take vengeance on His adversaries and repay those who hate Him. Behold, He will cleanse His land and His people."

Then, after saying all this, the city was silent, so the king surveyed all that was before him in silence, then he climbed down from the wall and walked among the people and they revered him, bowing and kissing his feet. He walked out to visit the site of his second captivity, and there, along the way, Cain met him. He spoke with him for a while, and they were a long way off. They touched not but Cain turned and walked away from him angrily, though the king tarried for some while. After some time, the king departed. We saw him not again.

THE CITY REBORN

Yet even as the king declared to worship The Creator and not The Watchers, soon the whole town was even more sinful than previously. And there was only evil continually, and they took every woman they saw to take, except my daughter Nammah, who they dressed with paint, and gave her gold to wear and kept her in the new temple they had built around the altar. They had put up new walls and painted them with depictions of themselves and their sons and their tokens which they carried. The rooms were fitted for their shoulders and tall head-dresses and their sons and sons-sons were multiplying and all the women we produced only served to mark their new conquest.

For Watchers returned in a seven-fold vengeance, and they had taken up residence in eleven other great cities and though ours was first, it stood cursed in their mind for the guardians of Tartarus had shown them what lay in wait for them on the other side of eternity. And so, Irad took control of the city and it became Eridu for Enoch and Irad, and they served continually in the ways of The Watchers and forgot everything that had befallen them.

And so eventually they came for Adah and Zillah and I could not stop them, for they were half HAdam and half seed of the king and they bore strange flesh to them, year after year. We could not take them away for they were captive in the ever growing company of flesh, and Lilith, Cain's wife was priestess among them and bore to Semjaza many children. But to Azazel she bore none, for in her turmoil she said: "His towers are overgrown with thorns and his fortress is a home for thistles!"

After a time Semjaza stretched forth his kingdom to extend farther and send envoys to make cities deeper and wider along the rivers and moved to Uruk, whom he had built for The Prince of Uruk, away from Leviathan who ruled the sea. Prince Uruk had come down from his silver mountain carrying his black ivory throne and ruled over the land.

Of my daughter Nammah, we could find her not, but reasoned later that she was in Teze or Nineveh, but some said Mauli and many others said Kish. But what was sure was that she was harlot to the gods and served under the Council of The Prince of Uruk, as his consort, though she remained childless no matter The Watchers that lay with her, such I would have no heirs from her loins and The Creator knows that I counted that as a blessing in my heart.

HEART OF STRUGGLE

So my sons were submissive to Mehu-Sael as he was to Mehu-Jael as he was submissive to Irad as he was submissive to Enoch. But for me, my sons submitted not, for I had forsaken the ways of the city and had gone back to the ways of the garden where there was only confusion, anger, and hatred for knowledge. But the love of knowledge was the root of all kinds of evil. And so, I sought wisdom in place of new devices. And pitched my tent not, for it was cumbersome and left it be to whatever winds might take it. And I built a hut near Cain and carved upon bricks the story of our city and I carved upon roots the incantations of blessings and of cursings so that I might trade in the city for food to eat.

But my forefather Cain took pity on me and gave me bread sopping in milk and gave me my own goat, so that I might have milk. And I bathed not, but carved all the day, and my teeth became rotten and all men reviled me.

Cain walked by my hut one day, and cursed, rebuking me that I stank like a score of camels, So he dragged me to the river and tossed me into it, wrestling away my clothes and letting them wash downstream. He gave me new clothes and commanded me to work in the field with him. Thus, after a while, I dwelt with Cain.

After some time, I came into my right mind, returned to my tent, after some repair, I interacted again with men, and in time, took another wife. And it was at that time that both Zillah and Ada returned to me and we had many other sons and daughters. But the heart of my struggle was with honoring both men and The Creator. For though I had risen again to prominence in the city and in all the land of Nod, I still trusted no man but Cain.

My oldest three children nor any of their descendants speak to me and so I made a good life with the latter children, of whom was seventy and three, for we sought to replenish the land in its whole. And of my wives, they each had three concubines who were counted among their own. And after a while, my sons built for me a house in the city that I might not dawdle out in the mud of the fields, and they burned Jabal's tent so that I was left with no recourse but to succumb to their will.

And the City loved me, after its fashion, and they demanded that I rebuild the ancient place of Semjaza, but I relented and let them build one to Armaros, who was our prefect and acted as a governor to us, for Semjaza and Azazel had naught to do with this City. But even Armaros or the other Watchers did not come to our gates, for it was etched into their memory still that the City of Cain, Enoch, and Irad, now called Eridu would not be touched. For even Enoch had left and only Cain, Irad, and myself remained. And Irad served at my behest, his mind being touched with the deep roots and leaves of incantations.

THE PRINCE FALLS

After some time, Cain came to the gates to see how I fared. And he had it in his mind to see the Prince, to see if he be worthy of his allegiance.

Then we set forth to see him in the City of Uruk, and I came alone with him, with a legion of my sons carrying the sharpest weapons, for my eldest sons were twelve times more hostile towards everything to do with our City and would have naught to do with us. But so they would not kill us, we brought our insurance.

Then Cain banged upon the city wall but they would not have us until Prince Uruk stood on the wall and rebuked us. And the city wall was high, higher than 20 cubits and there was only one gate and it was shut against us. We clamored outside until Prince Uruk came.

He spoke to us saying: "Who are you foul creatures of the old world here to vex the new? For you are not on the old holy ground but upon the new chosen ground. When I met you many cycles of Nanna hence, did you think I would recoil back into my seat up on yon mountain, unknowing and unthinking and unseeing all that you have done? For you had a city that was founded in the mysteries of The Watchers and you destroyed it, claiming that you now have a secret oracle of the old master and now seek to dethrone me here in my newest seat!? For my seat shall reign a thousand times ten thousand years!"

Upon his head, he bore a mark, though it was not the mark of Cain but a Pe with two Ayin, so it read: "Ayin, Pe, Ayin." Saying, "Eye, Mouth, Eye" or "Those I see, I eat." This was the mark of Uruk and of The Watchers and it was not holy but stood for the seeing and doing of sin. Prince Uruk was changed also, upon his face and eyes were many metalwork hoops, puncturing his skin and around his mouth and he was vile and turned around, lifted his skirt and relieved himself on our heads, so we left then, knowing that even The Watchers could corrupt the Princes of the Council.

Thus saying, he left abruptly and there was a commotion on the other side of the top of the wall and another man, taller but of a dimmer light within peered over at us. His helm was that of a reindeer, dipped in blood. And it was the thirteenth son of Bezaliel, who was brood of Watcher, and who held the city in his own mystery and who poisoned the ears of Prince Uruk against all of man.

And I called to him saying: "We have come here to speak words only to your master, and not to the men sitting on the wall, who are destined with you to eat their own dung and drink their own urine!" To which he left and Prince Uruk returned and I proclaimed to him the very words of The Creator, for, as I spoke, I felt a sweetness fill my very soul and something like a burning brand upon my tongue, but it was as cool as morning honey.

PROPHESY AGAINST THE PRINCE

"Your pomp has been brought down to Sheol, along with the music of your harps. Maggots are your bed and worms your blanket. How you have fallen from heaven, oh morning star, son of the dawn! You have been cut down to the ground, destroyer of nations."

"You said in your heart: 'I will ascend to the heavens; I will raise my throne above the stars of The Creator. I will sit on the mount of assembly, in the sides of the north. I will ascend above the tops of the clouds; I will make myself like The Creator.'"

But you will be brought down to Sheol, to the lowest depths of the Pit. Those who see you will stare; they will ponder your fate: 'Is this the man who shook the earth and made the kingdoms tremble, Who turned the world into a desert and destroyed its cities, Who refused to let the captives return to their homes?'"

"But you are cast out of your grave like a rejected branch, covered by those slain with the sword. Dumped into a rocky pit like a carcass trampled underfoot. Prepare a place to slaughter your sons for the iniquities of their father. They will never rise up to possess a land or cover the earth with their cities."

And having thus prophesied to him, I left.

Cain, however, tarried outside the city until they opened the gate to him and he stayed with him doing deeds I did not know.

And so, taking my sons with me, I went home to my family and stayed there in contentment.

THE CURSING OF BENE-ELOHIM

The song Zillah, of Lamach:

Elongated of form,
Beauteous in body.
His wood shavings are rotten shavings of the palm.
The snake waits coiled in the dwelling,
The serpent waits coiled among the rushes.
As for the serpent, two are his heads,
Seven his forked-tongues, seven the parkulla of his neck.
I smote the parkulla,
Yes even the parakulla,
Nahash the forest snake,
Leviathan the snake that cannot be conjured away,
Even Tiamat, who does battle with the one summoned against her!
Swift-kneed, fast-running, distorted by hunger, short of food.

In their teeth they carried their semen:
Wherever they bite they leave their offspring.
Oh El, lord of living,
He asks for my life.
Take him away that I might live
As the plow impregnates the earth,
Enki enchants himself,
Let me enchant myself and let me cast a spell!
Enlil enchants himself.
Let me enchant myself and let me cast a spell!
Annunaki enchants themselves,
Break me free from their power forever.
The sheep and the lambs are seized,
They are seized.
They smite the hip, so they cannot run.
Arise El and smite those that smite the sheep.
Arise El and smite those who smite the hip.
Yes El, strike my enemies on their jaw!
Oh El! Arise and break the teeth of the wicked!

ADAM REVISITS

One day, after many years had gone away, early in the morning, king Adam came and sat at my porch at the gate of Irad, where I often broke my fast. He had in his hand a water skin and he motioned me to wash my feet and so I let him, for I did not know it was him, as he was dressed in a simple white ephod and had radiant white hair and a flowing beard. I took him for a simple man, wishing to bless an elder.

But when he beheld me, face to face, I knew it was the king and I bowed low and worshiped at his feet. He picked me up saying that such an act was not to be, but he simply wished to visit an old friend and to see if I had come to worship The Creator once again.

But after the years had taken their toll on me, I confessed to him all that I had done. That I had given up and lived still in the shadow of Cain, as a servant, but that now I was the prince of Eridu, small city though it was, proud and first. And he asked me of my old family and I confessed that my eldest sons were said to journey here and there and once Tubal came to Eridu but saw me not. And I knew not of my eldest daughter or my first wives.

The king stayed with us for another coming of Nanna, not willing to leave, wanting to extoll The Creator in my presence and help with the governance of the city. But nothing was as he liked. For there was a great sin in the land, such that he wept so often, it was daily. But to me he begged that I could make the changes so that people would not sin so greatly. He begged time and time again to tear down the altars to the other gods but I was complacent and dwelled not on it choosing to drink wine and barleymash.

After all the carnage and bloodshed that he and I had seen here so long ago, his mind was very still, though his breath came in quick breaths when he would remember cleaning this or dragging certain bodies to be burned there.

For we burned all the sons of The Watchers the Guardians had killed. We had cleansed the city with fire. But of the guardians, the king asked time and time again and we told him what the Ophanim and The Prince had told us and he pondered these things. He had seen many but they ran from him, so he could not get close. They feared no man, but only men of the garden.

And we saw not the guardians nor his kin around any city of man, but they had moved into the great forests. And they interfered not with the wars of the Watchers. And we gave them the name of Humbaba and some of them were now living in them near Eshnunna, for it was there that the men called them the Humbaba, guardians of the souls of Ishtar.

And king Adam, having his fill of his visit, blessed us with his words and left us.

And Cain knew that his father had visited and came to watch us daily with covetousness in his heart but remained far away and did not approach, though he appeared as a wild man on the earth.

THE WICKEDNESS OF EARTH

I dwelt and ruled in Eridu in the shadow of the second man of earth, my father's father, Cain, who bore the mark. I, his seventh, also bore a mark upon my head and I showed it proudly. Cain, having given his turban up, shaved his head like me and would come visit me time and again. He brought news of this and that, and would sit and talk until he fell asleep in his barleymash and wine, telling me stories of the wide world, for I never left Eridu. He talked to no one but me in those days, for no one would talk to him. He was a reminder of things that no one wanted to put in their mind, and I alone remained his friend.

And so, the king's fifty and six children began to multiply on the face of the earth. And they became as dust in the wind and some moved to the cities Cain built but others became wanderers far to the east and some far to the west while others visited Eridu rebuilt whose name had become Irad and the city that was once Enoch and the people of Cain from then on co-married with the people of the king and of Seth and of each other and The Creator saved for himself a remnant.

And because of the Watchers and their brood, the children of the king soon became as corrupt as the children of Cain when they settled with them, such was the great sin over all the earth. For in every city that they dwelled, there was a Watcher or one of his children. And they went to the deserts and the seas and the high places and low places. Only the king's third son remained pure before The Creator.

And Watcher fought over Watcher for territories here and there and great wars were waged upon one another, for anger and rage fueled them in all that they were. And great beasts were bred among the greatest cities of the Watchers, and great spires and towers were built, to rival the others. And they built great ships to sail all of the seas and they built steppe towers, one after another so that they might have the entire earth as their kingdom.

And the sin of Cain happened as oft as one drinks water.

And they created for themselves great myths and fantasies. In the great city of Thinis, they made for themselves castes of the Nephilim, great and mighty so that they might wage war upon them of Bashan. And the ha-Satan of Hermani and Turiel took great chariots into Bashan that they might overthrow the Watchers of that region and they were thrown asunder by Gadreel, the mighty who had with him the brood of Kokabel. And they took Hermani and Turiel to Dudael to be held in chains but Raphael forbade them to keep them there and so they took them to the great Archons that dwell on the edge and shackled them together by the feet of them, so that they would be frozen forever.

And all the ha-Satan's hated each other and ruled their small lands, ever destroying one another. And The great Ha-Satan was rampant in those days, eating whom he will, going this way and that, befriending one Watcher to only turn on them by betrayal and mating and cavorting with all he chose. And though he was cast down into the erets, he dwelled in the great sea and was away from the minds and hearts of man.

But The Creator was silent and men did as they pleased. But The Word was seen in those days, moving here and there with a throne of Jasper seated above His Ophanim, moving where He would and recording the foul deeds of the hadam and the Watchers and their brood, the Nephilim.

And more and more wickedness was poured out on the earth and only king Adam and still his third son Seth remained pure before The Creator.

THE VOICE OF THE WORD

And so all the hadam and sons of Adam began to multiply over the face of the whole of the earth. They ventured to the sides of the north and to the most eastern and western places. They traveled south and over the seas and mountains.

And the Watchers took men and women everywhere and their seed was continually abounding over the whole of the earth. And they built their towers and their steppes to their great selves and to the Watchers and it was told that they devoured all who stood before them.

And it was the year of Jubilees, and The Word of The Creator came in the voice of the Seven Thunders and I heard a voice uttering over all of the earth, and the whole of the earth shook with The Word and it said:

"My Spirit shall not contend with hadam forever. He is now made mortal and his days shall be now one hundred and twenty years."

And there was a great darkness that fell over the land and it was dark for the time it takes Shemesh to travel a cubit in the vault. And all The Watchers and their sons and the daughters of all and also the sons of all men were sore vexed. But when the darkness was lifted, men began to do again what they had always been doing.

But the Spirit of The Creator was no longer dancing on the face of the waters, but sought hard for a people to worship The Creator in spirit and in truth.

LAMECH VISITS EDEN

Of my salvation I know not where it lay, for I have ventured far and wide and come to no new knowledge of how to become one of the elect. Though I spoke with the tongues of angels, I had not love, and I was nothing. Though I had been an instrument in the hand of The Creator, I was like the chaff which the wind blew away. I was nothing, and I knew it. I was of the bloodline of sin and there was no hope for me. Still, I had to know this wisdom in my face. I could not take rumors on the wind.

That my eldest sons have never ceased following in the teachings of The Watchers is obvious to me that I cannot reach them, except perhaps Tubal, so I sent word to Nineveh where he lived that he might visit me once again before He and I left this earth. And he was a mighty warrior before The Lord of Hosts.

And so I brought him with me to visit Eden and find out what could be done about our very souls. But as we approached we grew very afraid and could not approach. For in our minds we beheld two fiery sons of The Most High Creator and they had flaming swords to devour all who approached, so we pitched our tent there by the gates of the garden of Eden to see what we would see.

And Tubal-Cain was obedient to me and I asked him to take me to the river that we may bathe together so that we might purify ourselves there and enter therein and become one with The Creator. And Tubal-Cain did as I asked, though it was obedience and not agreement, therefore he submitted to me, his old father.

And after we bathed and consecrated ourselves there, we built a little altar but we had nothing on it to burn so it seemed good to us that we might hunt the forest to the east of Eden for a sacrifice to The Creator there.

And so we foraged for game there and when we spied a wild boar, we both took aim with our bows and shot. Both arrows struck the beast true.

And a cry like that of a man pierced the air.

THE END OF CAIN

The arrows that had been struck the wild boar had not hit a boar but they had found their mark on our forefather Cain, who lay wheezing blood as we came to him. And we knew not why he had been there, dressed in furs, like that of a beast and we turned him over.

And he declared to us: "I so desired to commune with The God of the garden." And then there was a great fit of coughing from him. "But this is my just return on my sin." He looked at me and my son deeply and then said: "That Abel's blood has claimed me with the man seventh born from me, and his heir, who bears my name." And then he spoke no more.

His turban was gone and his marks were red and flaring upon his wrist and forehead and, there, as we held him in his last breaths, the marks on his body shone brightly, then disappeared, for he had died.

And I looked at my son Tubal, and he stared at me, but the marks we had made on our heads and hands had not left us, for they were inflicted by my own hands and not the hands of The Word of The Testimony, nor by The Lord of Spirits.

And so we wept greatly for the second man from the garden, the first man ever to have been born on earth. Cain, son of king Adam, son of The Creator.

And we took him back to the altar, there, by the gates of the garden of Eden, and we laid him upon it, and we let the flames devour him.

And behold, as his body was consumed, the blood from the earth cried out and the earth groaned and there, before us, the garden of Eden fully faded from view.

And my son Tubal-Cain and I tarried there not a moment longer, but we left the altar and the consumed body and the strange signs that we saw and we wandered for a while before camping where we lay to sleep, as dead men.

And on the morrow, I found that Tubal-Cain had made his own way back, abandoning me in my misery, and thoughts.

And I stayed in that place until Sabbath, hoping beyond hope that Eden might return.

When it did not, I found myself and ventured home.

LAMACH WRITES

All the things that have happened to me I have carved long on the tablets, for here now in my old age I dwell not with men. I have carved them upon the tablets and have done this time and again and buried them now here in this silver mountain where The Prince dwelled. There was a cave near where the Ophanim opened our eyes to the vision. You will find these here. Also you will find copies in Lagash and Sippur and also Nineveh. Along the Tigris and Euphrates I have buried these, with some stories not told, for my hands are frail now and can no longer carve at any long length.

My wives have gone to Susa. My sons have moved to other cities. All that is left is old Irad who lays in a bed all the day, his mind awash with herbs. My son's sons knew not where I had gotten, only that I left at night, carrying nothing but my tablets, heavy though they be. You will not find this last tablet among the others, for only this tablet remains with me.

And so ends my journey. Though I know not if the tales be true, but I hear that one of the king's sons has another son and has named him after our line. As well as another Enoch, there is another

Lamach. I would be lying to you if I told you anything, however, I pray to The Creator that his seed prospers in all that they do.

Maybe someday come this new Enoch or Lamach will teach his sons and son's sons the way of good, for all is lost to me. I have given up the way of righteousness, for I do not know how to have it, nor have I ever. I recall briefly, as a youth, watching one of the daughters of the hadam being taken by one of the Watchers against her will and thrown down and ravaged. This is my first memory for before that time I had no memory. Perhaps my first memory of sin was when I ceased knowing what was sin.

Therefore I have sacrificed to The Creator and I have sacrificed to Semjaza. I have sacrificed now to Cain and king Adam and I have sacrificed to the Prince who is in Uruk. I am tired of sacrificing to these men and elohim. If I have found one thing to be true, is that they are all silent towards me and all hold their faces far away. I will build another altar to The Creator, and see if one last time He will hearken to me and hear my cry, or will the sins of my people and my very hands lay in wait as a snare against me.

I know that I have seen the power of The Creator for when I visit the hidden forests I see the great shaggy beasts... The guardians. They are a dim light of the glory of The Creator, but they are dim beings altogether, leading not into salvation, but guarding the gate of death. But that I saw their release upon the land, I may praise The Creator for HIs kindness towards me and the sons of men. But of His love for me, I know not.

These are the words of Lamach, seventh from the king, son of the garden. The king bore Cain who bore Enoch who bore Irad who bore Mehu-Jael who bore Mehu-Shael who bore me who bore me three sons of import. Jabal and Jubal and Tubal, who is of Cain.

These are my words and they are true.

www.ingramcontent.com/pod-product-compliance
Lightning Source LLC
Chambersburg PA
CBHW051926220626
47052CB00003B/593